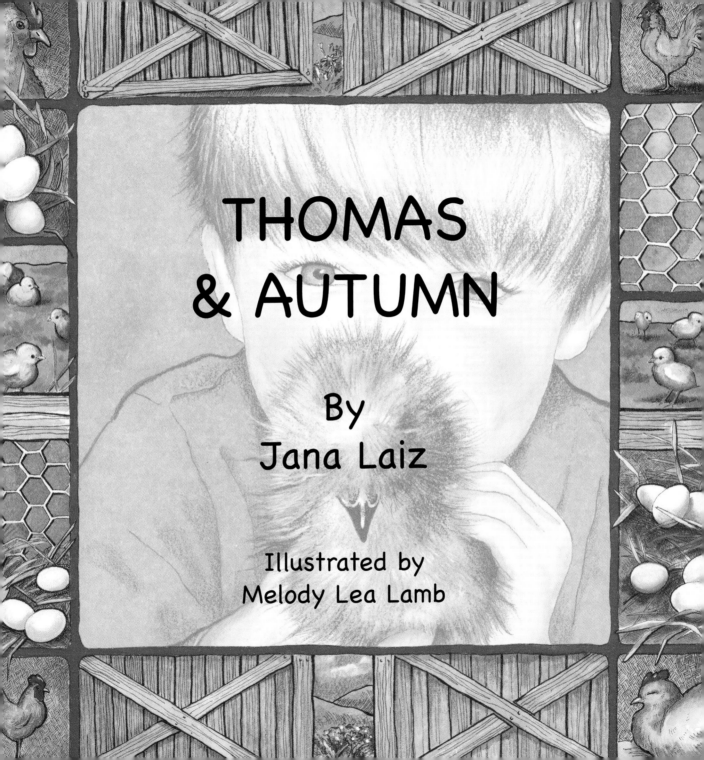

THOMAS
& AUTUMN

By
Jana Laiz

Illustrated by
Melody Lea Lamb

Published 2013 by Crow Flies Press

Library of Congress Cataloging-in-Publication data is on file with the publisher.

send all inquires to:

CROW FLIES PRESS
PO BOX 614   SOUTH EGREMONT, MA 01258   (413)-528-3856
www.crowfliespress.com
publisher@crowfliespress.com

ISBN # 978-0-9814910-9-7

First Edition

Dedications:

"This book is dedicated to two very special beings; Thomas, the lovely boy I have known since the day he was born and to Autumn, the very special chicken who brings joy wherever she goes." J.L.

"I dedicate this book to all the precious animals who have yet to find their forever homes." M.L.L.

Many thanks to the following organizations for their support, direction and encouragement:
   Berkshire County 4-H and Poultry Judges Astrid and Wanda
   NEPC Youth Program
   APA-ABA Youth Poultry Club

To all those who shared in Autumn's adventures:
   Cameron House
   Construct
   GBRSS Kindergarten
   Hancock Shaker Village
   Kimball Farms
   Old Parish Church
   Seashell Motel
   Sheffield Farmers Market
   Sheffield Kiwanis

To those who cared for Autumn through her life:
   Dr. Caine at Bilmar
   Kristen of the Trailblazers 4-H Club
   Sandy and Sabrina of the Fantastic Farmers 4-H Club

Also by Jana Laiz:
Elephants of the Tsunami, Weeping Under This Same Moon,
The Twelfth Stone, "A Free Woman On God's Earth"

This is Thomas.

He is six years old.

Today is a busy day for Thomas. He is going to the Northeastern Poultry Congress to look for the perfect chick.

Thomas has five dollars to take to the show. He has worked very hard for his money. Here is how Thomas earns his money.

Every morning Thomas follows Mum to the barn. Thomas feeds the chickens and the ducks.

He collects eggs from the chickens.

"Hello girls," he says to them. "Thanks for the eggs!"

He brings the warm eggs back to the house, trying hard not to drop even one. He carefully washes and dries them and gently places them in an egg carton. When he collects a whole dozen he puts them in a cooler in his front yard with a little sign he made. "Eggs for Sale - $1 a dozen."

People like fresh eggs.

Thomas has to go to school, so he leaves his money can out by the eggs. Everyone is honest and leaves just the right amount.

When Thomas gets home from school, he runs out to see what is at his egg cooler. He always hopes the eggs are gone and his money can is full. It has taken Thomas some time to earn enough money to buy his very own chick, but the day is finally here.

He and Mum pile into the station wagon and head to the show. Thomas would like to buy a Silkie Bantam chick. Thomas knows that Silkies are the gentlest of all chickens. They are very sweet and easy to tame. Thomas wants to win blue ribbons. He has already won several ribbons with his other chickens at the 4-H fair. He likes hanging them up in his room. Mum and Dad are proud of Thomas.

The Northeastern Poultry Congress is a bustling place. When they arrive, Thomas stops just outside the entrance and looks around. Downy feathers are in the air and the sound of peep-ing and clucking is everywhere.

He grabs Mum's hand and in they go. Inside are rows and rows of cages filled with show birds. Thomas has one thing in mind and makes a beeline for the chicks. And good thing too, for there is only one Silkie left, the runt of the brood. This little one is so fluffy it is hard to see where her eyes are.

Thomas picks her up and she nuzzles into him. He goes up to the woman selling the chicks.

"How much for this one?" he asks politely.

"She's seven dollars. Do you have that much?"

"I have only five dollars," Thomas says with a little frown, but Mum hands him two more dollars. Thomas looks gratefully at Mum. He will work extra hard to pay her back.

"Now I do!" he says with a big smile.

"Then you may buy her."

Thomas hands the woman the money and the chick is his! He holds her gently as they walk around the show, and then, after he finishes the last of his French fries, Thomas places the drowsy chick into his empty carton. She snuggles down into it and falls asleep.

It is late by the time they get home. Thomas is not tired. He wants to play with his new chick. But Mum calls, "Time for bed Thomas and little chick."

"All right," Thomas says.

For all his hard work in the barn, Thomas' mum has bought him a cage and a heatlamp so he can keep his chick in his bedroom. He places her carefully into her new home and she settles right down on the soft shavings. Thomas climbs into bed, and turns to watch his baby fall asleep. After a long time, Thomas sleeps too.

15

16

The next morning, the chick is up early, making soft peeping sounds. Thomas likes those sounds. He scrambles out of bed and goes right to the cage.

"Good morning!" he says cheerily. "Did you sleep well? I must think of a good name for you!"

Thomas has thought of many names for many chickens. He has named Jupiter, Petunia Truffles, Sunshine, Skippy, Peep and many more. He will think hard about this very special chick.

It is time for school. Thomas cleans the cage and gives his chick fresh water to drink and scratch to eat. He says goodbye and leaves for kindergarten. He will tell his teachers and all his friends about his new little chick. When Thomas gets home from school he tells Mum that he has named the chick.

"What will you call her?" Mum asks.

"Autumn! I will call her Autumn!"

"What a beautiful name. How did you come up with that?"

"We were talking about seasons today in school and Autumn is my favorite."

19

Thomas and Autumn
are becoming good
friends. They do many
things together.

Autumn follows Thomas
into the barn to help collect
the eggs. She says hello to
Jupiter. Petunia Truffles comes right over
and introduces herself.
All the other chickens like
Autumn. She clucks and
peeps in a friendly way.

21

Tuesdays are soup days at Thomas' school and Autumn is invited to come and join the class. The children busily chop vegetables to add to their soup, but instead of com-posting the scraps, Autumn gets them. What a special treat! After soup time it is naptime. Thomas puts Autumn back into her traveling cage and she rests too. When it is time to wake up, Autumn helps the teachers and uses her gentle clucking as an alarm clock to wake the sleeping children. The children look forward to Tuesdays and so do Thomas and Autumn.

Thomas and Autumn are best friends. Autumn waits for Thomas to get home from school and clucks excitedly when he opens the door. Autumn joins in when Thomas and his friend Olivia play together. Thomas reads books to Autumn. Autumn has become part of the family. Autumn brings joy to everyone she meets. People smile when they meet her at the nursing home, at the county fair, at the farmer's market, even at the Walk for the Homeless.

One hot summer day Mum announces they are taking a holiday. They are going to the beach.

"Can Autumn come?" Thomas asks.

"Sorry Thomas, she can't stay in a motel," Mum says.

"Well then," Thomas says, "I will stay home."

Mum has an idea. She knows Thomas will be unhappy without Autumn, so she finds a motel that takes pets. "It's a chicken," she tells the man on the phone. "A what?!" he says. "A chicken."

"Well I'll be! The rule says we take pets. It doesn't say what kind. I guess you can bring your chicken. It'll be the first one, ever."

Thomas and Autumn build sand castles and play in the sand. Thomas and Autumn ride in a paddleboat. Autumn watches Thomas while he swims in the ocean. Everyone is amazed to see a chicken on the beach.

It is time again for the Northeastern Poultry Congress. This year, Thomas is bringing Autumn to show. Autumn looks very fluffy and poised as Thomas stands with her before the Judge. Many other children are showing their special chickens.

"Please show me her feet," the Judge tells Thomas. He holds Autumn up and shows her fluffy feet. "And her wings, please." Thomas pulls gently on Autumn's wings and she helps by stretching them out. The Judge nods her head and smiles. Some of the other birds are fidgeting, but not Autumn. She is calm and still. Thomas has trained her well.

31

When all the children have shown their chickens, the Judge makes her decision. "Thomas, Autumn, please come forward." Thomas looks at Mum and Dad who give him a nod and a smile. "Thomas, congratulations, you win first place in showmanship. A blue ribbon for you and Autumn."

Thomas is proud of his little chicken. He loves her. And Autumn loves Thomas too. Everyone can tell they are special friends. Thomas and Autumn will have many more adventures, you can be sure.

The End

Jana Laiz has been writing for as long as she can remember. She is the author of the Award Winning novel, *Weeping Under This Same Moon*, Moonbeam Silver Medal Winner, *The Twelfth Stone*, *Elephants of the Tsunami*, and the co-author of *"A Free Woman On God's Earth."* She is a teacher, a writer, an editor, a mom, an animal lover, a sea glass collector, a musician and a dreamer. She is the very first Writer-In-Residence at Herman Melville's beloved Arrowhead. She lives in a 200-year-old farmhouse in the Berkshire Hills of Massachusetts with 2 kids, 2 dogs and 2 cats.

Is Melody an artist who can also talk to animals - or a lover of fur and paws who also draws like a dream? The combination has led to some interesting life circumstances, from teaching art in a chicken coop to composing watercolors on horseback. Having done her time at art school and the gallery scene, Melody now paints miniatures in the Berkshire Hills while tending to a husband, a horse, three cats, two kids, and a dog.

Thomas is a real boy who lives in Massachusetts and keeps a flock of about 50 egg laying hens. As well as his love for chickens and caring for any animal in need, Thomas enjoys hiking, surfing and playing team sports. When not outdoors he has a keen interest in antiques, music and reading.

Autumn is a real Blue Bearded Silkie Bantam hen raised by Thomas and loved by many for her unique and endearing personality.